SMARTY the BRAIN stories

SMARTY **MOODY**

by Brian S. Hamilton

Archway Publishing books may be ordered through booksellers or by contacting:

Archway Publishing
1663 Liberty Drive
Bloomington, IN 47403
www.archwaypublishing.com
844-669-3957

Illustrations by Daniel Majan

ISBN: 978-1-6657-6121-5 (sc)
ISBN: 978-1-6657-6122-2 (e)

Library of Congress Control Number: 2024911613

Print information available on the last page.

Archway Publishing rev. date: 06/28/2024

Contents

To my family and friends,
who got me through the dark
days after my brain injury

Note to Parents:

This book is intended to act as a safety storybook to be read to preschoolers. The stories teach them to use safety strategies to protect their brains. Once children begin reading, they can use this book to make safe practices a fun part of life.

Smarty the Brain

Smarty was a young brain in elementary school. He liked playing with his friends, riding his bicycle, going to the movies, and eating his mom's spaghetti. He was very friendly and helpful.

One day while riding bikes with others, a brain named Moody pushed Smarty, who fell and hit his head! Smarty always wore a helmet when he rode, so he wasn't hurt, just a little shaken up. Moody thought it was funny and laughed; he never wore a "dumb helmet".

The next week it was raining, and Smarty carefully rode his bike to school. His helmet was keeping him warm, dry, and safe. As he pedaled on the sidewalk, he saw Moody riding too. Moody had no helmet, just a baseball cap.

At a cross street, Moody darted out onto the wet road. Smarty stopped at the curb just as Moody wiped out in front of a car! The car screeched to a stop just in time to avoid a crash.

Smarty parked his bike, looked both ways, and ran out to help Moody. Moody had been almost knocked out when he hit his head on the road and was speaking odd words with a strange voice. A woman came up and said she was a doctor. She asked Moody his name, and he seemed to snap back into reality and answered slowly.

After a quick exam, the doctor got Moody out of the road. They heard a siren, and soon an ambulance came. The medical team took Moody to the hospital, where doctors examined him and found he had a concussion. His mom came to get him.

Meanwhile, Smarty continued to school, but he couldn't stop thinking about Moody and wondering whether he would be all right.

After school, he went to Moody's house and rang the doorbell. Moody's mom came to the door and told him that Moody was home but his head hurt and he was resting. So maybe Smarty should come back tomorrow.

The next day after school, Smarty was able to see Moody, who was very sorry that he had been so unkind. He asked Smarty to teach him how to be safe so he wouldn't hit his head on the street anymore.

Smarty gave Moody many lessons on how to protect himself and keep his brain safe. They even discovered some safety methods together. This is why the two became best brain buddies!

Moody Misses His Seat Belt

One day, best brain buddies Smarty and Moody were visiting Smarty's cousin, who was going to take them for a ride in his pickup truck. His cousin and a friend were in the cab, so Moody and Smarty went to the cargo bed.

Moody said, "Hey Smarty, there are no seat belts here. It's not safe."

Smarty replied, "Right, Moody!" He then called to his cousin and told him about the problem.

His cousin replied, "You know, you're right, especially since we'll be taking a bumpy road. Let me drop my friend off; then I'll come back and get you. You two can sit in the cab with me and use seat belts."

While Smarty's cousin was taking his friend home, Moody said to Smarty, "Wow, I messed up, didn't I?"

Smarty said, "Why do you think that?"

"If I hadn't worried about the lack of seat belts, we'd be having a fun ride now," said Moody.

"And maybe getting hurt, Moody," said Smarty. "You never know when bad things can happen, so it's best to stay safe."

So Moody's quick thinking and speaking up saved both of the best brain buddies! They really enjoyed the bumpy ride wearing seat belts with Smarty's cousin.

Smarty and the Baby Gate

It was a rainy day, so Smarty and Moody were playing at Smarty's house. Smarty's baby brother, Bernie, was able to crawl but not walk yet, so Smarty's mom and dad had put baby gates at the top and bottom of the stairs so Bernie wouldn't fall.

Moody said, "Hey, Smarty, this gate sure makes it hard to walk down the stairs."

"That's the idea," said Smarty. "But you see this foot pedal here? The gate opens fast if you use that. It's only for a couple of years, while Bernie's not so good on his feet."

Moody didn't have any siblings, so he wasn't familiar with baby gates. But he learned about them from his friend Smarty. So when his aunt brought home his first baby cousin, he was able to tell his aunt and uncle about them. They installed baby gates on their stairs while they were babyproofing their house.

A few months later, Moody and Smarty were playing games at Moody's house when Moody's aunt stopped by with the baby cousin. "The gate saved your cousin, Moody! I wasn't watching for a second, and he would have fallen down the stairs if not for the gate."

Moody and Smarty felt proud that they had helped save the little brain from falling.

Moody and the Battery

Moody didn't have any siblings, so when his aunt brought his new baby cousin to his house, he had to learn fast about kids. One thing he learned was that small children tend to put things in their mouths.

He was playing on the floor with the baby while his mom and aunt talked in the other room. He noticed that his aunt had left her purse on the floor, and there was a bottle of cough syrup in it that the baby was interested in. Luckily, the bottle had a childproof cap, so the baby couldn't open it.

Then Moody noticed that the TV remote was also on the floor; somebody must have accidentally kicked it, and the small battery was falling out. He saw his cousin trying to put the battery in his mouth, so he ran over to the baby and grabbed the battery just in time. He gently corrected his cousin to keep things out of his mouth.

His cousin started crying when Moody ran over to grab the battery, so his aunt looked in from the other room and saw Moody consoling his cousin. "He was going to put the battery in his mouth," said Moody.

His aunt said, "Oh my! Well, you have saved him twice now, Moody. You deserve all my thanks."

Smarty the Skier

When Smarty was a preschooler, his parents asked him whether he would like to go skiing with them. He had no idea what it would be like, but he was excited and said, "Yes!"

The first thing to do was get equipment for him. At the local rental shop, his mom and dad asked the boot fitter to help them find the right boots for their son. This was important for comfort and skiing safety. After the boots were selected, the fitter suggested skis and fit the boots to the ski bindings.

Then came a very important piece of equipment: a ski helmet. They also got goggles to protect Smarty's eyes, and they put the goggles on the helmet.

Ski day was beautiful but cold, so Smarty dressed in his snowsuit before going to the ski hill. There he put on his ski boots and his helmet. His parents helped him take his skis to the base area, where he put them on and tried skiing around a little. He felt great!

Then his mom and dad took him to the beginner hill, and he followed his mom's suggestions to put his skis in an upside-down V shape so he could control his sliding. He slowly slid down the small hill, and he was feeling awesome. Smarty got on the small chairlift, went to the top of the beginner hill, and skied down again and again and again. He was rapidly improving and having a great time.

Smarty's dad suggested they ski over to the bigger lift, and Smarty was eager to try. He wasn't moving very fast across the flat snow yet, so Smarty's dad pulled him along with his pole.

They got to the chairlift, and it was big enough for all three of them to get on at once. They enjoyed looking at the sights as they rode to the top of the hill. Once at the top, they skied over to a trail marked with a green circle, for easy.

Smarty's dad went first down the hill, then Smarty, and then his mom. They went slowly so Smarty felt comfortable. Smarty followed his dad's turns, and he was really enjoying himself—until his ski got caught in an icy rut and he fell over. As he fell down, he hit his head on the ice; it felt like someone had punched him in the head!

He was shaken, but because of his helmet, he was OK. His mom and dad came to him and made sure he was all right, and the three of them decided to go in for a break.

While in the lodge, his mom asked him how he felt. He replied that he had a slight headache, but it went away after he had some hot cocoa and a sandwich.

The three skied a couple more runs, and all was well. Smarty really enjoyed his first day of skiing!

Moody and the Slide

Back when Moody was a tough guy and didn't care about anybody else, he would hang around the playground and push other kids to get feelings of power. Moody didn't realize that he could be doing permanent damage to others; he just didn't think about it.

One day it had been raining, so everything was a little slippery. Moody showed up at the playground in time to see a couple of brains using the slide. They thought it was great because it was so slippery.

Moody stood by the slide as the brains came down and pushed the others so that they would fall off the slide. This wouldn't be so bad if the slide were on grass or soft rubber matting, but it was on concrete! The brains fell face-first onto the unforgiving surface. Not only were kids getting bloody noses, but also there was unseen damage being done to their young brains.

Finally, one brain came to the slide, stood up to Moody, and made him quit abusing kids on the slide. He was able to show Moody that people could really get hurt by hitting the concrete under the slide. So Moody finally realized that his actions were just wrong, and he had his first encounter with Smarty.

Smarty and the Skateboard

Moody and Smarty saw other kids riding skateboards, and they wanted to try it. Smarty thought he could ask his parents for a skateboard, since his birthday was soon. Moody said with caution, "Isn't there some safety equipment we should also get?"

Smarty researched it on the internet and found out that the American Academy of Orthopaedic Surgeons recommended this safety equipment for skateboarding:

- Properly fitted multisport helmet
- Close-toed, slip-resistant shoes
- Wrist guards
- Kneepads
- Elbow pads
- Goggles or glasses

"Whoa, that's a lot," said Moody.

"Better than getting hurt!" exclaimed Smarty. He also learned that since skateboard riders fall a lot, they should learn to fall safely.

"Here's how to fall safely," read Smarty, still looking at the computer. "If you feel like you're about to lose control, crouch down so you don't have as far to fall. Try to land on the fleshy parts of your body. Try to roll rather than absorbing the force with your arms, and try to relax your body rather than going stiff. Practice falling on a soft surface or grass."

"Wow!" said Moody. "Lots of ideas." Moody also read, "Check your equipment before skateboarding. Your skateboard should not have loose, broken, or cracked parts; sharp edges; a slippery top surface; or wheels with nicks or cracks."

Smarty read from the computer screen, "Stay safe rules: the American Academy of Pediatrics cautions that children younger than five should not skateboard at all, and children ages six to ten should not skateboard without adult supervision. Obey local laws. Never ride in the street. In a multiuse area, skate on the right side, pass on the left, and be cautious of others using the same area. In skate parks, be considerate of other skateboarders, especially those younger or less skilled. Don't use headphones when skateboarding. Never put more than one person on a skateboard, and don't get pulled by a car or bike."

"Well, I guess since we're both seven, we will need our parents to supervise us," said Moody. "Now let's go have fun practicing falling … in the grass."

Buddies Play Baseball

It was April, and the Little League was starting to practice. Moody had been on the team for a year and was excited to play shortstop. He asked his best brain buddy, Smarty, to try out for the team, and he did. The coach asked Smarty to be the catcher, which involved wearing a lot of equipment. A helmet, a face mask, kneepads, a chest pad, and a big glove were all intended to keep him safe from flying balls and sliding players.

The first practice involved a lot of running and batting. They learned that batters *always* wore helmets, even when they were just running the bases. This was to keep them safe from thrown balls. In their age group, a pitched ball could travel almost fifty miles per hour!

Finally, the next week they got to practice their positions. There were two pitchers for the team, Tommy and Jose, and Smarty put on his equipment and practiced catching for both of them. Moody practiced catching and batting, and in the last half hour of practice, they had a game.

When it was time for Moody to be at bat, he walked up to home plate and looked at his friend Smarty. Smarty said, "Go, Moody!" Moody smiled and turned to look at Jose, who was pitching.

The pitch came in, and Moody hit it toward center field and ran. He made it to first base while another player ran in from third base and collided with Smarty, who had just caught the ball from the second base player. The runner was out, and Smarty was a mess, but he was all right because of all his safety equipment.

Horseback Helmets

Smarty and Moody got an invitation to ride horses at a nearby stable. Since the trainer was a friend of Smarty's mom, Smarty had seen a lot of the ponies, but he had never had an official riding lesson.

They first learned that as with most other sports, having the right equipment is important. A riding helmet held on by a chin strap protected against falls, and riding boots helped riders control the horse's speed. Finally, having a properly trained pony was a must because the animal could weigh up to eight hundred pounds. For safety the pony needed to have a calm demeanor.

Smarty and Moody chose helmets that were hanging from a rack. They needed to fit well—not too tight or too loose. Then the chin strap had to be comfortable. So they each tried a few before finding one they liked. For this first ride, they could use their tennis shoes, but in the future the trainer told them they should get riding boots.

The trainer introduced them to the ponies she had chosen for the brains. They walked the horses over to the mounting stand, a small platform with stairs to help them get on the ponies. There they each got up in the saddle, and the trainer adjusted the stirrups so their feet sat well.

Then they were able to ride around the training paddock, and the trainer gave them pointers on how to show the ponies which way to go by gently pulling on the reins to turn the ponies' heads. The trainer also told them that to go faster, they should gently kick the animal's side and make a clicking noise; to go slower or stop, they should pull back on the reins and say, "Whoa."

Moody and Smarty enjoyed riding horses and wanted to come back. They were really glad to have learned the basics of horsemanship and some safety rules.

Smarty and the Snowmobile

It had been snowing for many days, and the best brain buddies were tired of being in the house. Smarty's dad said, "Hey, boys, let's go for a snowmobile ride on Saturday."

Smarty was excited, but Moody didn't know what to expect. So Smarty made sure that his friend had the right equipment: a snowsuit, boots, gloves, a helmet, and goggles.

On Saturday morning the weather was bright but cold. Moody and Smarty got dressed in their snow equipment and met Smarty's dad in the car. It was a short drive to the snow park, where there was a snowmobile reserved for them.

Smarty's dad drove the snowmobile, and the two small brains sat on the seat behind him. Moody said, "But there are no seat belts!"

Smarty's dad answered that the reason for the missing seat belts was because they were surrounded by snow, and if there were a problem, they needed to be able to leave fast! It was the same reason there were no seat belts on a motorcycle.

They got moving slowly at first. They followed an established trail, and it was a smooth ride. Then Smarty's dad said, "OK, boys, let's open it up!" They entered a straight section of the trail.

"Wooooooo!" screamed Moody and Smarty together.

They got to the end of the straight trail and were still going quite quickly when Smarty's dad turned fast so they made the corner. Smarty almost flew off the snowmobile; only Moody grabbing him from behind kept him on board!

They soon got over the excitement and had a fun, safe ride through the rest of the trails. At the end, Smarty thanked Moody for making sure he wasn't thrown off. So the best brain buddies learned all about snowmobiling and how to do it safely.

The best brain buddies continued on with Smarty's dad and had an awesome ride on the snowmobile. At the end they made a pact to go again!